How I Love You, Daddy

For Dad

Scholastic Canada Ltd.
604 King Street West, Toronto, Ontario M5V 1E1, Canada

Scholastic Inc.
557 Broadway, New York, NY 10012, USA

Scholastic Australia Pty Limited
PO Box 579, Gosford, NSW 2250, Australia

Scholastic New Zealand Limited
Private Bag 94407, Botany, Manukau 2163, New Zealand

Scholastic Children's Books
Euston House, 24 Eversholt Street, London NW1 1DB, UK

www.scholastic.ca

Library and Archives Canada Cataloguing in Publication

Pignataro, Anna, 1965-, author, illustrator
    How I love you, Daddy / written and illustrated by Anna Pignataro.

Previously published: Australia: Scholastic Australia, 2016.
ISBN 978-1-4431-5731-5 (hardback)

    I. Title.

PZ7.P614586Ho 2017   j823'.914   C2016-904603-6

6 5 4 3 2 1   Printed in China LFA   17 18 19 20 21

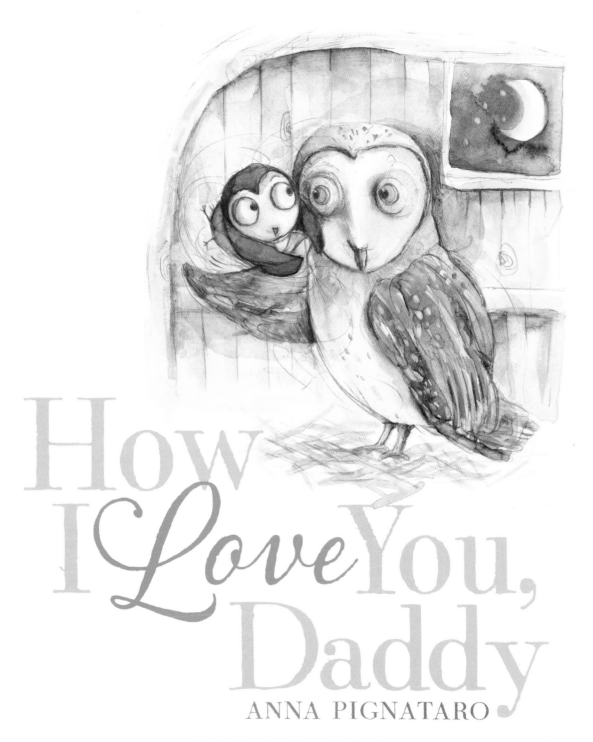

How I Love You, Daddy

ANNA PIGNATARO

Scholastic Canada Ltd.
Toronto New York London Auckland Sydney
Mexico City New Delhi Hong Kong Buenos Aires

Under the Milky Way,
three little tigers were tumbling with Daddy.
Three little tigers blew raspberries and said,
"This is how we love you, Daddy."

Little Polar Bear was chasing
Daddy over the snow.

Little Polar Bear nipped Daddy's neck and said,
"This is how I love you, Daddy."

Baby Hedgehog was rolling in a shrub.

Baby Hedgehog bounced on Daddy's tummy and said,
"This is how I love you, Daddy."

Little Elephant was playing in the river.

Little Elephant splashed Daddy and said,
"This is how I love you, Daddy."

In the emerald leaves, Little Red Panda was hiding.

Little Red Panda pounced on Daddy's shoulders and said,
"This is how I love you, Daddy."

Little Wild Hare was jumping
higher than Daddy's ears.

Little Wild Hare wrestled Daddy and said,

"This is how I love you, Daddy."

Baby Blue Penguin was sloshing in a pool.

Baby Blue Penguin dived onto Daddy and said,

"This is how I love you, Daddy."

Little Barn Owl was flying to the moon.

Little Barn Owl swooped high and low over Daddy and said,
"This is how I love you, Daddy."

Under the Milky Way, it was time for three little tigers to go to bed.

Daddy nipped,

bounced,

splashed,

pounced,

wrestled,

dived,

swooped,

and blew raspberries
on his three little tigers.

"And that is how I love you," he said.